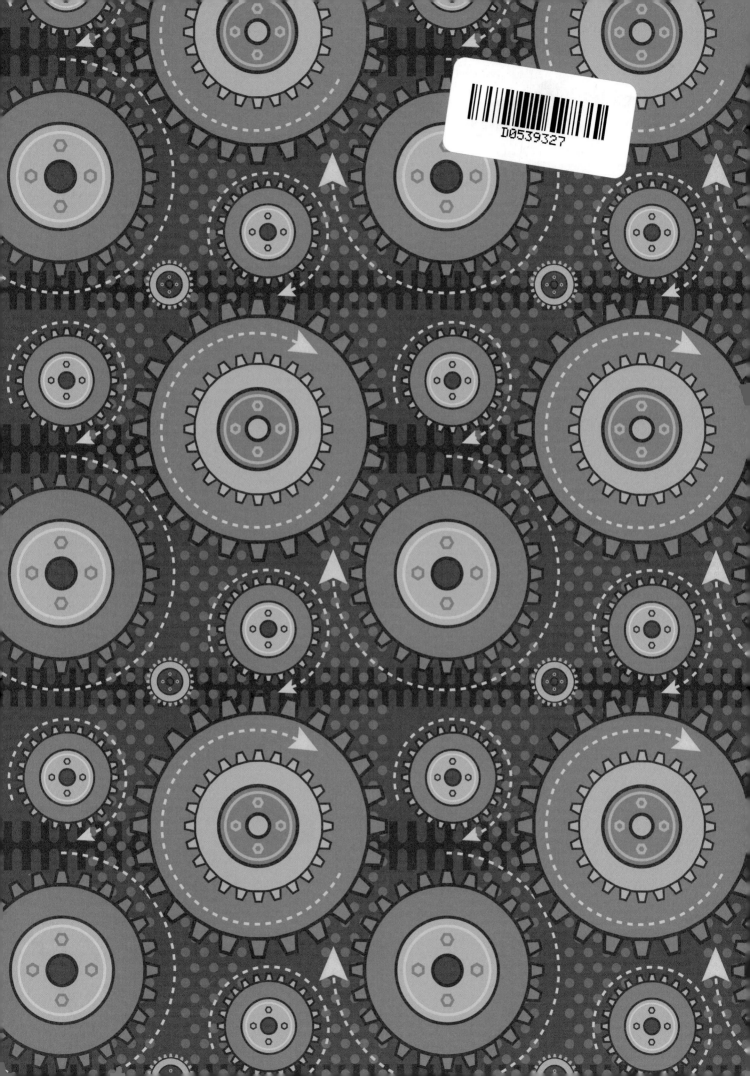

This Bob the Builder Annual belongs to

....

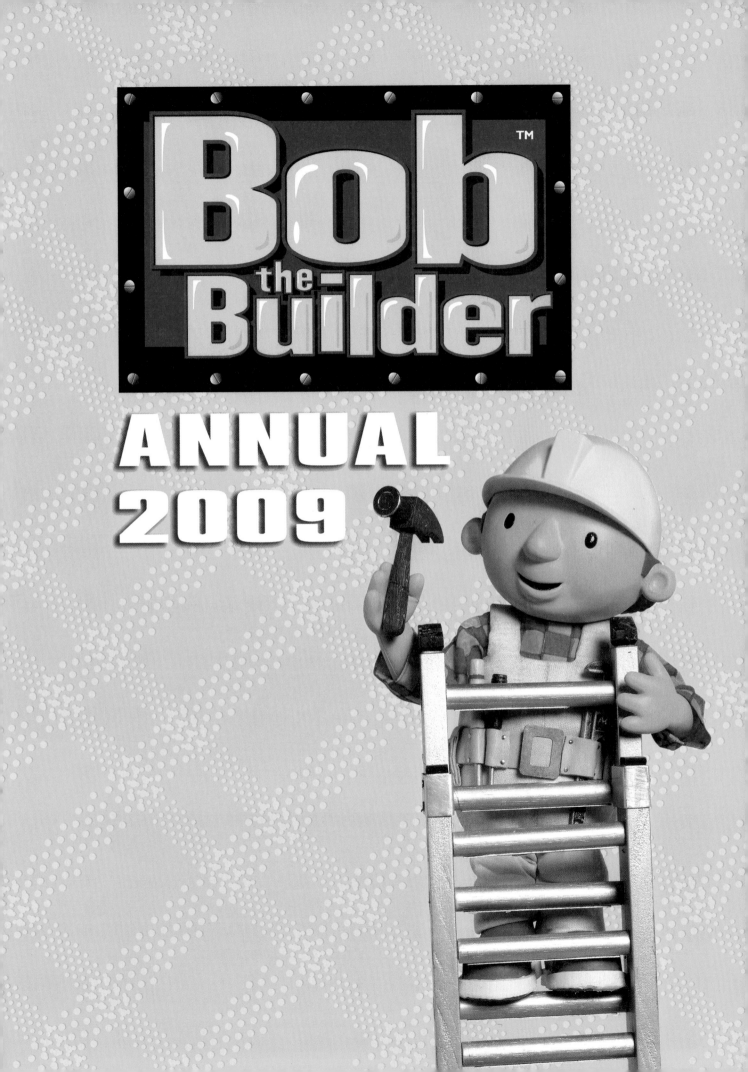

Contents

First published in Great Britain in 2008 by Egmont UK Ltd, 239 Kensington High Street, London W8 6SA

EGMONT
We bring stories to life

Based on the television series Bob the Builder © 2008 HIT Entertainment Limited and Keith Chapman.
All rights reserved. The Bob the Builder name and character, related characters
and the Bob figure and riveted logo are trademarks of HIT Entertainment Limited.
Reg. U.S. Pat. & ™. Off. and in the UK and other countries.

Written by Brenda Apsley. Designed by Sally Seeley.

ISBN 978 1 4052 3915 8
1 3 5 7 9 10 8 6 4 2
Printed in Italy

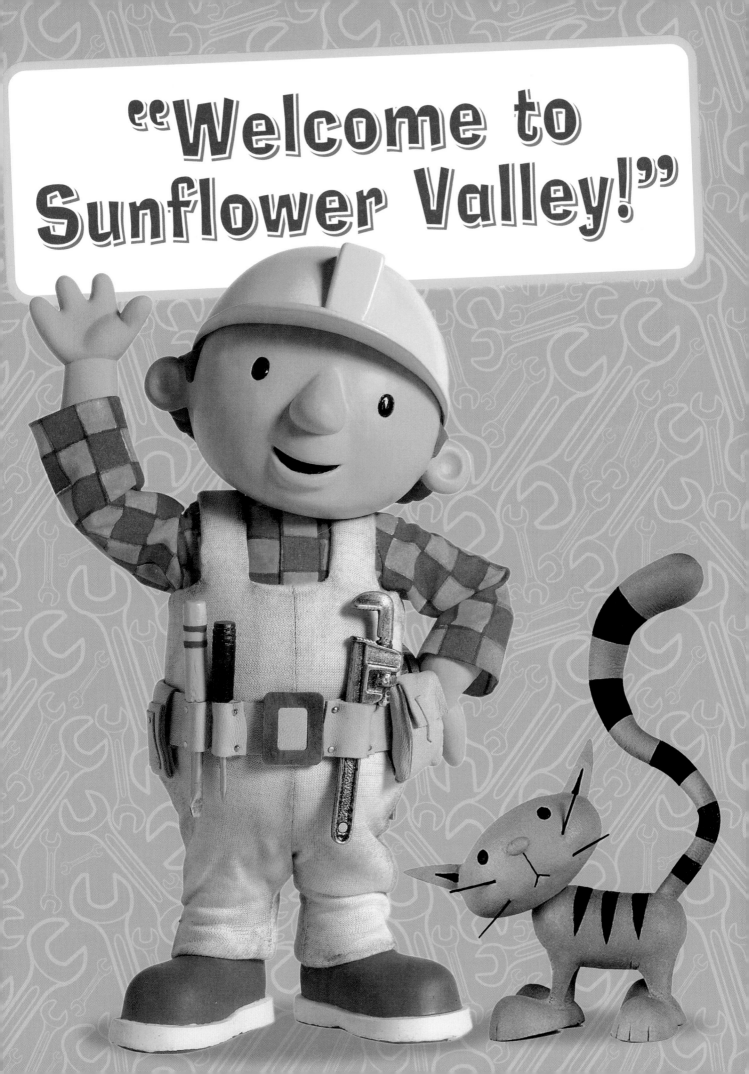

Bob the Builder

Bob is a very busy builder who can build and mend all kinds of things.

Bob used to have a building yard and an office in Bobsville, where he grew up. Now he has a new yard and a new mobile home in a new town called Sunflower Valley!

The homes and buildings are all 'green', which means that they are built using materials that can be recycled and reused. They are built in a way that reduces the effects of building on the plants, animals and birds in the valley, and they use 'green' energy, like power from the sun.

"There are three words to remember," says Bob. "Reduce, reuse and recycle!"

Bob fits equipment that saves energy.

Bob plants new trees to replace the wood he uses.

Bob decorates with recycled wallpaper.

Bob's Team

Bob couldn't do the work he does without having a great team to help him.

Bob's work partner, **Wendy**, makes sure that everyone has the materials and tools they need.

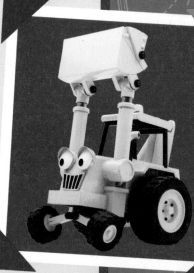

Bob's pet cat, **Pilchard**, is not a builder, but she IS an important member of the team!

The leader of Bob's machine team is a yellow digger called Scoop. He's good at moving dirt around, and digging big holes!

Bob's green steamroller, Roley, has two big rollers which he uses to smooth out rough ground, and to flatten roads and paths.

Dizzy is Bob's orange cement mixer. She uses her big spinning tub to mix cement, concrete and plaster for the team.

Bob's blue mobile crane, **Lofty**, has three special tools: a magnet, a grabber and a demolition ball. He uses them to do all kinds of useful jobs.

Muck, the red digger-dumper, just loves being mucky! He does all the really messy jobs like dumping, digging and moving earth around.

Scrambler is a blue all-terrain four-wheel drive vehicle who can travel over rough, bumpy ground, carrying things in his trailer.

The youngest member of Bob's team is **Benny**, the pink robo-digger. He has attachments including a drill, a hammer and a six-in-one shovel.

Friends and Neighbours

Bob has lots of friends and neighbours in Sunflower Valley.

Farmer Pickles lives at Scarecrow Cottage with his pet dog, **Scruffty**, and **Spud** the scarecrow. He keeps animals on his farm, and grows sunflowers in the fields. He has a green tractor called **Travis** and a fork-lift truck called **Sumsy**. Spud's job is to scare away crows like **Squawk** from the sunflower fields.

Marjorie looks after the sunflower factory. Sunny and Saffron are her children.

Mr Sabatini and his family moved from Bobsville. He makes flour for the Sunflower Valley Bakery.

Mr and Mrs Bentley live in a house in a hill.

Sandy Creek knows all about dinosaur fossils.

Mr Beasley lives in a yurt house. He grows all kinds of fruits.

Ela Stevenson is a teacher. She likes playing the drums!

Sumsy's Willow Tree

One day, Travis, Sumsy and Scruffty were playing hide and seek.
   When Sumsy found Scruffty hiding in his kennel, it made her think. "Travis, why haven't we got a shelter?" she asked. "Scruffty's got one and Bob's machines have, too. I'm going to ask Bob to build one for us!"
   Just then, Bob and Lofty arrived to help Farmer Pickles move an old willow tree that had fallen over.
   "It won't be wasted," Bob explained. "We can use the wood for lots of other things."

"Good," said Lofty. **"Reduce, reuse, recycle!"**
Farmer Pickles got Sumsy to load equipment
and crates on to Travis' trailer, then they drove
to the riverbank.

Lofty moved the old tree, then Bob and
Farmer Pickles cut up the trunk into big logs.

When Spud arrived, Sumsy told him about the shelter. "I want to ask Bob
about it," she said. "But he's too busy …"

"No need to ask Bob!" said Spud. "Scarecrows are good shelter-builders!
I'll build it using those logs!"

"But they're the logs Bob and Farmer Pickles cut," said Travis. "What if
they need them?"

"Nah, they're just old logs!" said Spud. "Bob will be pleased if we make something out of them! **Reduce, reuse, recycle,** remember?"

Sumsy and Spud took the logs to a clearing, and began building. But before long, the shelter fell down, and so did Spud!

When Sumsy went back to the riverbank, she met Farmer Pickles. "Have you seen those logs, Sumsy?" he asked. "We need them to make fencing."

"Oh, I'll get them!" said Sumsy, racing back to the clearing.

"Sorry, Spud," she said. "Farmer Pickles needs them!"

When Sumsy delivered the logs, Bob split them, and made a frame. Then Farmer Pickles wove flat bits of willow through it, to make a fence panel.

Sumsy found a crate of thin twigs. "As they're no use for a fence," she said to Travis, "will you take them to Spud for our shelter?"

But just after Travis sped off, Wendy arrived. "Sumsy, have you seen a crate of twigs?" she said. "I'm going to use them to make a broom, and Mr Bentley is going to make a basket."

Oh, no! Now Sumsy had to bring the twigs back again.

Soon, all that was left were the empty crates. "That's it!" said Sumsy, and she took them to the clearing.

"We can use these to build a shelter!" she said. "No one needs them."

"Yessity-yes!" said Spud. "A crate shelter!"

But Sumsy was wrong! Wendy needed the crates for her broom and Mr Bentley's basket. But where were they?

Bob and the others found the crates in the clearing.

"So this is where our things are, Spud!" said Bob.

"Don't tell him off," said Sumsy. "Spud's only doing what I asked him to. He's making a shelter for Travis and me. I wanted to ask you earlier, Bob, but you were too busy."

Bob smiled. "Well, I'm not too busy now," he said. "We still have the wispy bits of tree. But how can we join them together?"

Sumsy knew! "You could weave them together, like knitting a woolly jumper!" she said.

"Yes," said Bob. **"Can we weave it?"**

"Yes, we can!" said the others.

"Er ... yeah ... I think so," said Lofty.

With everyone helping, the shelter was soon ready, and Travis and Sumsy went inside.

"It's so cosy!" said Sumsy. "We used every bit of that old tree, didn't we?"

"Yes," said Bob. "We **reduced, reused** and **recycled**."

Farmer Pickles showed the machine team a little package. "It's a baby willow tree to replace the old one," he said. "I'll plant it, then put this cover around it to protect it."

"Now we all have shelters!" said Sumsy. "Even the baby willow tree!"

Scruffty the Dog

Scruffty loves bones! Draw 5 more for him to chew on, and colour in your picture as neatly as you can.

Pilchard the Cat

Pilchard loves fish! Draw 6 more to make her purr, then colour in your picture.

Slow Down, Scrambler!

One morning, Bob had an exciting new job for the team. They were going to build a bridge across the river.

"Oh, man!" said Scrambler. "Can I be the first machine to cross the bridge, Bob? Can I? Pleeeeease?"

Bob smiled. "I suppose so," he said. "I'm going to work on this side of the river, and Wendy will work on the other. Dizzy will be working with Wendy, so you can take the bags of cement for her. Make sure you cross the river at the ford. It's a long way round, but it's the only safe place to cross, where the water is shallow."

"Right! I'll go on ahead!" said Scrambler, zooming off. "Dizzy's too slow!"

"Hey, speed isn't everything!" said Dizzy, racing after him.

Scrambler and Dizzy hurried along – until Dizzy skidded off the path into some muddy ground! She called out to Scrambler, but he was too far ahead to hear her.

When Scrambler arrived without Dizzy, Wendy sent him back to get her.

Scrambler found Dizzy stuck in the mud. "Why didn't you call Bob on your talkie-talkie?" he asked.

"Because it fell in the mud," said Dizzy, angrily. "You'll have to go back and tell Bob what happened."

But Scrambler had other ideas! "Getting Bob will take too long," he said. "I'm going to get Wendy instead! I'll get some rope from her, then pull you out. It'll be quicker, and I can still be first across the bridge."

Scrambler went so fast that he didn't see two big rocks, and ran right over them. His trailer tipped over, and the bags of cement fell into the river. "Oh, man!" he said.

Work on Bob's side of the bridge was going well. Wendy, though, was still waiting for Dizzy to arrive with the cement, so Bob called Dizzy on his talkie-talkie. When there was no reply, he and Lofty set out to look for her.

Bob and Lofty soon found Dizzy, and Lofty pulled her out of the mud.
"What happened, Scrambler?" asked Bob.
"I was coming to get you, Bob," said Scrambler. "Then I thought I'd get Wendy instead. I was rushing … and … the cement's in the river … and … you were right, Dizzy, speed isn't important. I've made a big mess of things! I'm really sorry."
"The bridge isn't going to be finished today, is it, Bob?" said Lofty.
"No, Lofty, I don't think it is," said Bob. "Come on, let's go back to the yard for more cement."
"Oh, man!" said Scrambler.

Bob and the team worked really hard, and it was dark by the time they went home that night.

Next morning, Lofty lowered the bridge into place.

"Hurray!" cheered all the machines.

Bob and Wendy tied a red ribbon across the bridge. "Come on, Scrambler," said Bob. "It's time for you to be first to cross the bridge."

"Oh, man!" said Scrambler. "No, Bob, I've got a much better idea! I want **Dizzy** to be the first machine to cross the bridge!"

"I'd love to!" said Dizzy.

"Wicked!" said Scrambler. "Does that mean you forgive me?"

"Of course I do!" said Dizzy.
"Can she cross it?" said Scoop.
"Yes, she can!" said Dizzy happily, as she broke the ribbon and rolled across the bridge.
Then Scrambler crossed the bridge and stopped next to Dizzy.
"Friends?" he said.
Dizzy whizzed around happily. "Friends!" she agreed.

Speedy Scrambler

Colour in Scrambler using the small picture as a guide. These are the colours you need.

"Let's scram!" says Scrambler. Can you show him which path to take to get to Wendy? Remember, he can only cross the river at the ford.

Ford

Sir Muck

One morning, Bob was telling the machine team about their new job. "We're building a house for Mr Sabatini," he said.

"Can Spud come, too?" asked Muck. "He's telling me a story about castles and knights!"

"OK, Muck," said Bob.

As Muck rolled along, Spud read the story. "Then the knight came," he said, "and rescued the princess!"

Bob took the team to an old tower. The top part had fallen down, and there were bricks everywhere.

"The Sabatinis need a house near their bakery, and this will be perfect," Bob told the team.

"We'll be recycling the bricks from the old building," said Wendy.

"Muck, your job is to shift all the bricks to the new site," said Bob.

Just then, Mr Sabatini arrived on his motorbike.

"I really like this place, Mr Sabatini," said Muck. "It's like a castle, so I'll be one of your knights!"

"If I'm-a the king and you move-a the bricks, I'm-a gonna make-a you Sir Muck!" said Mr Sabatini.

"I'll help!" said Spud. "Then I can be Sir Spud!"

"Right," said Bob. "First we'll take down what's left of the tower, then Muck can move the bricks."

Muck worked hard, but Spud was more interested in his book. "Picking up bricks isn't a knight's job," he said. "But jousting is! Knights charged at each other with long poles, called lances."

"Like these?" said Muck, showing Spud some wooden poles he had found.

"Lances!" said Spud. "And these bits of canvas must be the tunics the knights wore!"

Spud climbed on to Muck and held out a pole. "Now we're knights, Muck!" he said. "Chaaarge!"

"Er, all right," said Muck. "But when we've finished jousting we'll move the bricks like Bob said, right?"

Spud and Muck charged, but they hit the bricks that Muck had piled up. The bricks fell everywhere!

"Spud!" said Muck. "It took me ages to collect those!"

But Spud took no notice. He showed Muck a picture in his book. "There's a knight who charged at a windmill," he said. "Let's find a windmill to fight!"

Bob and the team had fixed a wind turbine to Mr Sabatini's house.

When Spud saw its big sails turning, he pointed. "A windmill!" he said. "Chaaarge, Muck!"

As Muck charged, he knocked off one of the sails of the wind turbine.
"Oh, no! Now Mr Sabatini hasn't got any power for his house," said Lofty.
"Sorry," said Muck. "I've been really silly. I'll go and get the bricks."
The house was soon finished.
"It's-a fantastico!" said Mr Sabatini. "But is no-a power, and Mrs Sabatini and-a Carlo and-a Cassia are gonna be here soon!"
"Maybe the book will tell us what to do," said Spud, opening it at the picture of the windmill.
"Hey, this building isn't a castle," said Muck. "Look, it's a windmill! The lances and canvas are parts of the sails!"

Bob and Wendy made the poles and canvas into four sails, and Lofty lifted them into place. When the sails turned, the windmill would make power.

"Magnifico!" said Mr Sabatini. "Muck, for-a you, I 'ave a reward. From-a now on you are … Sir Muck!"

"Hey, what about me?" asked Spud.

"An' you-a can-a be Sir Spud," said Mr Sabatini. "But you gotta make-a one promise."

"What?" said Spud.

Mr Sabatini smiled. "No-a more jousting!"

"Chaaarge!"

Spud and Muck had a great time pretending to be knights!
These pictures look the same but 5 things are different in picture 2.

1

Can you spot them all?

ANSWERS: a cloud, a tree and Bird have appeared, one of the sails is missing, and Spud's shoe is a different colour.

Bashing, Crashing Benny

Bob   Benny   Muck   Scoop   Sandy

 has a new attachment.

"Now  can **bash** through

brick!" says 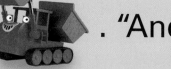. "And **crash**

through concrete!" says .

"He's Bashing, Crashing  !"

 wants to try out the new

attachment. But  has to see

 . "We'll try it out when I get

back," says  . But

can't wait!  wants to **bash**

and **crash**! The machines don't need

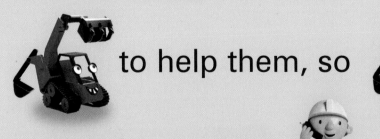 to help them, so

goes off to look for .

 sees a wall of rock. "I'll

bash and **crash** it!" says  .

But the new attachment does not

bash and **crash**. It just makes a

pattern. Suddenly, big rocks fall off

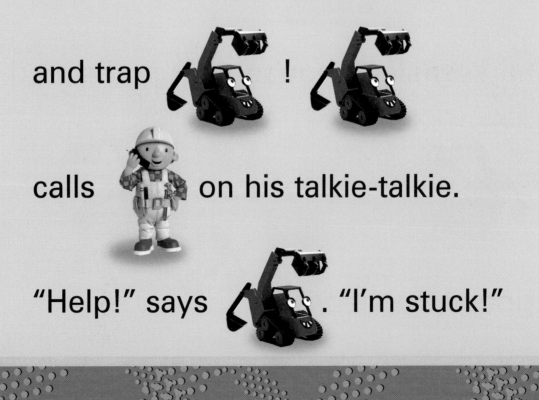

and trap !

calls on his talkie-talkie.

"Help!" says . "I'm stuck!"

and  rescue .

 sees a big dinosaur fossil in

the rock. "It's a good job you didn't

bash and **crash**, ," says .

"That would have broken the fossil!"

 smiles. "You're  the

dinosaur-digger!" says .

"Unreal, banana peel!" says .

"Help!"

Poor Benny! He was trying out his new attachment when big rocks fell down the mountain, and trapped him. It's a good job he had his talkie-talkie to call Bob! "Help, Bob!" he said. "I'm stuck!"

Which 2 pieces are missing from the jigsaw picture?
You can draw and colour them in if you like.

Bob's Top Team

One morning, Bob and the machine team set off for a new Sunflower Valley building called the Dome.

"It's going to be the new Visitor Centre," Bob told the machines. "We're going to build lots of displays inside. When people come to visit Sunflower Valley, they'll see what goes on here."

"And it's opening tomorrow!" said Wendy.

"But only little Dizzy can fit inside the Dome," said Muck. "What do you want the rest of us to do?"

"You're going up the mountain with me," said Bob. "Sandy Beech just called me from his cave. He says we can go and collect the big dinosaur fossil he found, and bring it here. It's going to be a special display."

"Can we fetch it?" said Scoop.

"Yes, we can!"

"Er … yeah … I think so," said Lofty.

"Hang on!" said Bob. "I've got to build the other displays first. Wait out here for me – I won't be long!"

Bob and Wendy worked really hard inside the Dome. There were lots of displays to build!

Outside, the machine team waited … and waited … and waited.

Hours later, when it was dark outside, Bob suddenly remembered about collecting the fossil! He went outside, but the machines were gone!

Bob didn't know where the machines were – but Scrambler did!

He took Bob to the bottom of the mountain, where they saw the machine team, Sandy – and the dinosaur fossil! – coming down the steep path.

"But how … ?" said Bob.

"I put my old lantern on Dizzy so she could light up the path," said Sandy.

"Roley flattened the path for us," said Dizzy.

"Then Lofty moved all the boulders," added Roley.

"And Sandy helped us load the fossil," said Scoop.

"Yes, we had to be very gentle with it," said Muck.

"You've got a great team!" said Sandy.

"Yes, a top team!" said Bob. "I should have let you get on with the job, instead of making you wait all that time."

"No worries," said Dizzy. "You can lead us the rest of the way."

Bob laughed. "You've done a great job without me, so I think you should finish it off on your own," he said. "See you back at the Dome, then we can all get some sleep before the big day tomorrow!"

Next morning, the Sunflower Valley Visitor Centre was almost ready.
Bob was hanging the dinosaur fossil from the roof when Mr Bentley
arrived, looked around … and smiled.

Mr Beasley stood beside his display of fruits, dressed as a pineapple!

Farmer Pickles' display showed all the animals on his farm. There were
pens of sheep and goats, and crates of ducks and chickens. And Scruffty
was there, too, of course!

Sunny and Saffron were helping Marjorie with her sunflower display.
It showed all kinds of things that can be made from sunflowers, like oil
and margarine.

Mr Sabatini's stall showed bread and cakes he'd baked using flour made at the mill, and Mr Bentley's own display showed how his house in a hill had been built.

Right in the middle of the Visitor Centre was Sandy's enormous dinosaur fossil.

"It's wonderful," said Mr Bentley. "Well done, Bob!"

"I couldn't have done it without my machines," said Bob. "We all worked together, as a team."

Just then, Dizzy rushed in. "The visitors!" she said. "They're coming! They're coming!"

"Let's show everyone what a very special place Sunflower Valley is!" said Bob, throwing open the doors. "I declare the Sunflower Valley Visitor Centre well and truly – OPEN!"

"Hurray!" said Dizzy, whizzing around. "Brilliant!"

Sumsy's Counting Fun

Sumsy loves counting! She had lots of fun counting the animals that Farmer Pickles took to the new Visitor Centre in the Dome. You can count them, too!

1 How many sheep can you see in the big picture? Write the number.

There are ☐ sheep.

2 How many goats? Circle the number.

1   2   3   4   5

3 How many hens? Colour in a hen for each one you can see, then count them.

There are ☐ hens.

Roley's Bird's-eye View

"Right, team, we've got a busy day!" said Bob one morning. "We're going to build an Observation Tower. Here are the plans. Visitors will be able to climb up to the top and see for miles across Sunflower Valley!"

"Like a bird?" said Roley.

"Yes, they'll have a bird's-eye view," said Bob. **"Can we build it?"**

"Yes, we can!" said the others.

"Er … yeah … I think so," said Lofty.

Scoop and Muck dug the foundations, then Bob, Wendy and Lofty built the main parts of the tower. Dizzy made a concrete floor and Roley rolled it smooth and flat.

Next, Roley and Muck made a path between the tower and the Dome. They were working hard when Bird, Roley's best friend, arrived.

"Bob's building a tower, Bird!" said Roley. "People will climb up as high as you birds fly, and see what you see! But I can't, 'cos I'm too big. I'll never get to see what you see."

"Toot!" said Bird. She wished Roley could.

"Lofty could have lifted me up the tower if I weren't so heavy," said Roley. When the path was finished, Muck and Roley went to look at the tower. Wendy and Bob had just finished the platform.

"It's amazing," said Roley. "I can't go up, so I need the view to come down to me. If Lofty held a mirror up high, I might be able to look into it and see the view from the top. Then I'll see what you see, Bird!"

Lofty held a big mirror in his grabber, and lifted it as high as he could, but it was too far away for Roley to see anything.

"Maybe you could use Bob's telescope?" said Dizzy. "It's for seeing faraway things. It has a special lens that makes things look bigger."

Roley rushed over to look at the telescope, but he couldn't stop in time. It wobbled, then crashed to the ground.

"Oh, no, what have I done?" said Roley. "I'm really sorry, Bob. I was hoping I could use a mirror and your telescope to see the view from the top of the tower."

"It's OK, Roley, it was an accident," said Bob. "But I think there is a way to make your idea work."

"In the old days, before there were photographs, they had a different way of seeing things. It was called a Camera Obscura, and it used lenses and mirrors," Bob explained.

"We've got a mirror!" said Lofty.

"And a lens from the telescope!" said Dizzy.

"The only other thing we need is a darkroom, a room with no windows, where we can see the picture," said Bob. "And we can build one of those!"

Bob and Wendy made a little darkroom at the bottom of the tower, then they built a big pipe that went up to the platform at the top.

Bob fixed the mirror and lens into position, then he took Roley into the darkroom. It was very dark when Bob turned off his torch!

Roley watched, and suddenly a perfect colour picture of the view from the top of the tower came all the way down the pipe and on to a white table.

"Oh-ho!" said Roley. "It's magic, Bob, magic! Now that's what I call a real **bird's-eye view!**"

Bob's Telescope

Bob can see all sorts of things through his telescope. It helps him see small things that are far away. You could look through it, too.

Which of these things can you see in the big picture opposite?
Tick ✔ ONLY the things you can see.

a

b

c

d

e

f

g

h

ANSWERS: a, b, c, f and g can all be found in the big picture.

59

Wendy's Houseboat

Bob had a very special job for the team. "We're going to fix up an old houseboat on the river," he told them.

"And I'm going to live in it!" said Wendy. "Come on."

The old houseboat was a real mess!

"Wendy's going to live in – THAT?" asked Scoop.

"It'll be fine," said Bob. "It'll be as good as new when we've finished with it. Come on, team. **"Can we fix it?"**

"Yes, we can!" said the others.

"Er … yeah … I think so," said Lofty.

Bob and the team put in new doors and windows, and repainted the houseboat. They put a solar panel on the roof for power, and fixed a gangplank from the bank to the boat.

"Finished!" said Bob. "Now all we need is Wendy!"

Back at the homestead, Dizzy was helping Wendy pack up her things.

"I'll look after Henny and Penny for you," said Dizzy.

"Thanks, Dizzy," said Wendy. "I'll show you how to feed them."

But Henny and Penny didn't eat any of the food Wendy gave them.

"That's odd," said Wendy. "They're always hungry."

"Cluck, cluck," said Henny and Penny.

"They sound sad," said Dizzy. "Perhaps it's because you're leaving."

Just then, Ela Stevenson, the new teacher, arrived, and gave Wendy a big envelope.

"It's a drawing of the kind of house I'd like Bob to build for me," she said. "Will you give it to him?"

"Of course," said Wendy.

Ela looked at Wendy's caravan. "Your caravan is really great," she said. "I've always wanted to live in one just like it."

"Yes, it's a brilliant place to live," said Wendy. "But I'm moving out today."

"You are?" said Ela. "Do you think Bob would let me move in? Then he wouldn't need to build me a house."

"I'm sure he wouldn't mind," said Wendy.

"Thanks, Wendy," said Ela. "I'll go and pack! See you later!"

Soon after, Scoop took Wendy to her own new house – the houseboat.

"Oh, it's lovely. Really lovely," said Wendy. "Thank you. All of you." Then she paused. "It's just that I'm really going to miss living at the homestead with you all. It's too late now though, because Ela's moving into the caravan. Oh, well, let's go and collect my things."

That night, Wendy sat on the deck of the houseboat, all alone. She couldn't sleep because the ducks were still awake, and they quacked … and quacked … and quacked.

"I didn't think you ducks would be quite so noisy," said Wendy. "I bet Bob and the others are fast asleep."

But Bob and the machines were wide awake, too! Ela was playing her drums, and the loud bangs and crashes went on … and on … and on.

Next morning, when Wendy went into the office, she found Bob lying on the floor in his sleeping bag.

"Why are you in here?" she asked.

Bob groaned. "Ela's drums," he said. "She played them for hours, and I just couldn't sleep."

"I didn't sleep much either," said Wendy. "The ducks kept me awake!"

Wendy gave Bob Ela's envelope. "I forgot this," she said. "It's a sketch for Ela's house."

"It's a houseboat!" said Bob. "Look, Ela wants to live in a houseboat!"

Can you guess what happened? Yes, Ela moved to the houseboat and Wendy moved back to the caravan!

"Welcome back, Wendy!" said Lofty. "We missed you!"

"Cluck, cluck, cluck, cluck," clucked Henny and Penny, happily.

Bob looked into their pen, and smiled. "It looks like Henny and Penny are glad you're back, Wendy," he said. "Look – they've made a present for you."

Inside the pen was a lovely big brown egg!

"Cluck, cluck, cluck," said Henny and Penny. Welcome home, Wendy!

Spud's Quiz

Can you help Spud with these questions? Look back through the book to find the answers.

1

Who is the youngest of Bob's machine team? Is it:
a. Scrambler
b. Benny, or
c. Scoop?

2

What colour is Travis the tractor? Is he:
a. blue
b. red, or
c. green?

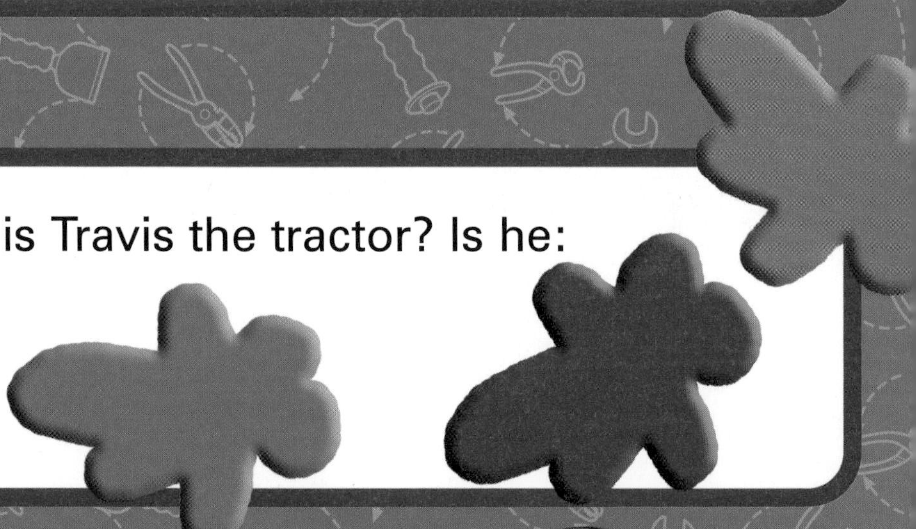

3

Who is this? Is it:
a. Mr Beasley
b. Mr Sabatini, or
c. Sandy Beech?

Is the name of Farmer Pickles' fork-lift truck:
a. Sumsy
b. Scrambler, or
c. Dizzy?

Who is this? She went to live on the houseboat Bob fixed up for Wendy. Is it:
a. Marjorie
b. Mrs Bentley, or
c. Ela Stevenson?

Bird is best friends with which member of Bob's machine team?
a. Scoop
b. Roley, or
c. Wendy?

See You Next Year!

"See you next year!" says Bob.
Colour in his picture as neatly as you can.

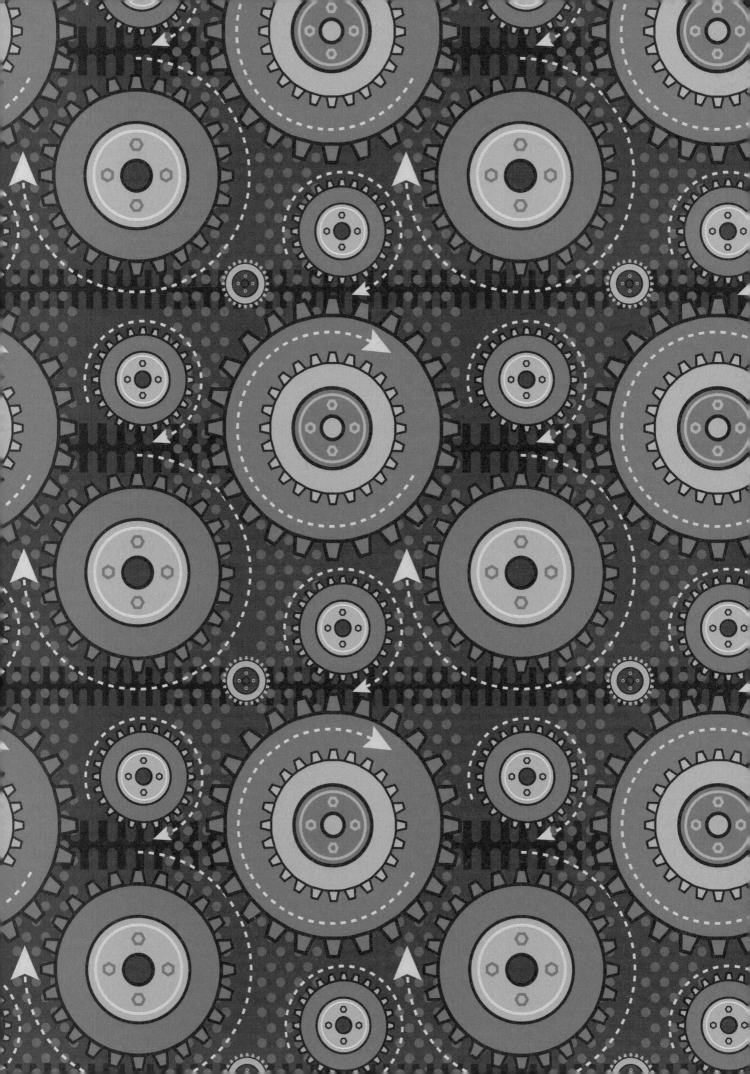